AF284528

S.E. Scheidl:

How I Lost 20 Lbs. and how I Saved GBP 100,00 every Fortnight
–
True Story of a Working Mum

DELECTARE – PURE TEXT SERIES – ONE RIDE-STORY
Volume 1

S.E. Scheidl

How I Lost 20 Lbs. and how I Saved GBP 100,00 every Fortnight

–

True Story of a Working Mum

DELECTARE – PURE TEXT SERIES – ONE
RIDE-STORY

Volume 1

Bibliographical data of the German National Library:
The German National Library records this publication in
the German National Bibliography; detailed
bibliographical data are available via internet under
http://dnb.dnb.de .

Editorial Office: S.E. Scheidl

Manufactured and published by: BoD – Books on Demand,
Norderstedt

ISBN: 978-3-7519-7654-1

CONTENTS

II

ENJOY YOUR SHORT RIDE

MAY A SMILE

BE YOUR COMPANION

DELECTARE – PURE TEXT SERIES – ONE RIDE-STORY

How I Lost 20 Lbs. and how I Saved GBP 100,00 every Fortnight

–

True Story of a Working Mum

FIRST ATTEMPTS

Well, how to start my amazing story best?

You know the feelings, the hunger for quietness, peace, time and a bar of chocolate. All this comes quite naturally if you have children. The younger the child, the more the chocolate will be you need…deserve…to overcome any problems, which trouble your mind: life, illness of the kids, birthday parties, school starting, kindergarten troubles…exhausting nights and days leaving you weary.

It might even be that you share your chocolate in some spare moments, bringing joy and happiness with a birthday cake, the first birthday… oh, until the 18th birthday comes…

Time is vanishing, life is vanishing, chocolate bars are vanishing, leaving you with some more pounds. Pooh, the scales must be wrong. Neither they are wrong, nor do they bewitch you with numbers you would like to see.

So what!

You say, time, chocolate and pounds are accumulating. The children, a boy, a girl, both you rear lovingly, working beside full day, you become a very soft mum, a rounder one. The children don't mind, they hug and embrace you with love even more, the rounder and fluffier you become. Bony mums are not that comfortable to share a bed with, when something aches, when a monster is hiding beneath the dark bedroom, lurking to frighten you…

But still…

But still…

But still…

Though you are a woman, you have just been a girl, you think, trying to catch a glimpse of your just temporarily lost figure in the bright and merry mirror, but giving you a rounder picture of your former self.

Well, time and energy you invest or have invested in your upbringing of your kids, your place in the working world, take their share of your youth and figure, even of your mind.

So, at several periods of time, let us say every 10 years, you realize you have to do something for YOU. Easy said, hardly done. What: Figure? Self-realization? You decide to approach the figure-issue. Might be the easier one, you will not get a big headache compared to the other issue, will you?

So did I!

When my children, a girl and boy, were 6 and 8 years of age, I invested a lot in very expensive pills one could by at the drugstore. Some worked, some did not. I started to eat less, especially in the afternoon and evenings.

But this is the time, you come back home to your family. They all are hungry. So are you. But you decided not to eat much or skip dinner. Your children, your family, of course do not want to skip dinner, they are naturally hungry. They are growing up, they need healthy food.

So, this obviously throws you into a conflict with yourself, your wishes and desires not to eat, but have to cook, bear the good smelling of fish, meat, vegetables, fruit, whatever...
In addition, you fear to be a bad or unhealthy role model for your family. This makes you feel very uneasy at the family table, in the kitchen, with your kids.

So, you start to eat a little, losing sight of your original plans, the scales won't go down then.
Well, nobody minds, but you.

So, then next 10 years later, you try it again. You may succeed or not. It depends partly on you. Losing weight might also be costly.

I have also tried to lose some weight, to look model-like and maiden again. Folks, I tell you, it is a hell of a lot of work to do. I tried to be consequent, having a small breakfast in the morning, eating a normal sized meal for lunch, finishing with an apple and much water at 4 p.m., avoiding really anything consumable afterwards.

But…

your kids are hungry…

waiting at home, ready for lunch…

What the hell to do? Honestly, I was not hungry after a certain period of time any longer in the afternoons, but I also could not stop to lose weight. I am not very fond of a bony figure and a haggard face, so I stopped eating those expensive pills, while keeping the afternoon-apple for dinner in my daily routine.

As I have already said, time goes by, chocolate lies within reach in the middle of your working space, placed there by a good soul of a working mate to inspire the afternoon work, the afternoon depression. That sucks!!!

Sure, I tried to restrain myself, avoid the way near the sweets, but as working hours got later and later, the more vulnerable I got…ending up at the sweets desk swallowing some sweets.

So, what? Life is short, but one must not end up straight in the sweets-snare.

It is not that easy then.

THE RANDOM PATH

Some years later I tried again.

It started almost by chance. I was out with my own mum, having a late lunch at a modest pizzeria. They presented a mother's menu that day, because the next day was mother's day.

The whole menu consisted of: bouillon with strips of pancake, main course: Wiener Schnitzel with French fries with salad, dessert: pancakes filled with jam. I was so sick then.

Something of this whole sumptuous menu did not do me any good. It was too much, too fat, whatever. My poor little stomach was aching and I could not eat much the next days. I also had to sacrifice my beloved cups of coffee. How terrible!

So, I remembered a good advice of my own mum of days passed by, to eat something very stomach-friendly and light, to please my poor aching stomach.

Therefore, I went to the supermarket, to our discounter, looking for some special products to find…
What I wanted to try out again was oat flakes or better rolled oates cooked with water and some milk.

Thankfully, I am not allergic against cow milk, though I only take some; just a dash, for my coffee. If I were, I would have also spared it. Well, but I am not, so I decided to cook some oat flakes, Let's say about 7 soup spoons full with some water and a bigger dash of milk.

Rolled oates should help my stomach to become fine again.

I tried to put up a routine. It is easier to put up routines at my working place. At home is it more difficult, the hungry family, kids surrounding me…

So, I decided to substitute my lunch, whatever I ate for lunch at work, by a plate of rolled oates. Well, what I usually bought outside for my lunch was not that healthy I suppose: something Chinese with rice from the noodle box, a kebup, a Schnitzel roll, a slice of pizza, sandwiches… This was really a censure in my lunch time at work!

My colleagues asked me suspiciously what kind of thing I would eat? Pooh, without sugar?

My boss, better one of my two bosses, met me in our tiny staff kitchen rummaging in the community fridge for his buttermilk. He really dared to ask me what I was that eating for and how long… I bravely told him that I have become one of my small projects, every bigger task I call a project until it is finished and I always finish my projects I tell you.

So, I told him that I had started with rolled oates for the better of my stomach. That I wanted to keep this routine in order to lose 20 pounds then. He was very astonished, raised his eyebrows and nodded benevolently. I told him that I just wanted to lose 20 pounds and look then what I would look like, because I do not like to be too bony then.

My boss was really impressed!

Well, that was the way I started:

Dinners I shared with my family, my kids. Only the lunches I skipped.

GOOD THINGS TAKE TIME

Time went by, one week, two weeks, three weeks, four weeks, skeptical glances at my cooking rolled oats in our staff kitchen at lunch time. Do you really like this? What do you eat it for?

Well, then it started: slowly. After a month or so, my colleagues and so did I realized that I looked somehow thinner. I was glad. I was motivated then and kept my lunch routine.

Four weeks, five weeks, six weeks then, nothing changed in my life, I only changed my lunch and kept the rolled oates routine.

Compliments became more and more, even when I did not tell everybody what I was going for. So, just by sticking to my rolled oates routine I managed to drop an entire dress size!

Wait, I also tried to keep my sweet tooth short and not to eat too much in the afternoon or for dinner, though I ate dinner with my family, my kids.

So, this was approximately after 5 months. I got really fond of my lunch because not only did I save calories with my modest meal, but I also saved money. Some spoons of oates, a dash of milk, water for free, some cents that just will be. So, some GBPs a day, more GBPs a week, a month…for … not for sweets…but for nice things, a shirt, a lamp, a carpet, a new chair, whatever.

So, instead of spending e.g. GBP 8,00 for one lunch, something Chinese, some fine Burger lunch, something pizza like…, you buy a pound of oates or let's say for about GBP 1,00 and one liter of milk (if you are not allergic) for about GBP 1,00. That will last for about 2 weeks.

So, if you just eat your rolled oates at your working place during the week, these are 10 meals within 2 weeks.

This means, calculating a very keen price your rolled oates meal costs about 20 cents. What a deal! You lose weight AND you save money. Saving just one ordinary working meal makes up the price for my booklet! What a deal! You pay less than the price for one amusing and authentic booklet!

However, when you want to try a diet or eat the same things I ate, you must consult a doctor in advance. This is very important! And this is nothing for kids or youths who are just growing up and need normal food to grow up healthy.

So, this is just my way, how I did it. It also might be just fun for you to read or to imagine.

OUTLOOK

For the time being I have stabilized my weight,
maintaining my weight, one entire dress size less…
In winter I may start again my programme a little tougher,
i.e. substituting my working lunch still for rolled oates and
be strict when being offered sweets, chocolate. Then I may
lose again another 20 lbs..

My dears, please be not frightened, I will not be too thin
then, but have a fine figure, ending up with 165 lbs. being
1.78 m tall.

I will tell you then.

SIDE EFFECTS

It is amazing, there are some other positive effects I realized when eating consequently rolled oates. Yes, in addition to the admiration of my boss and my colleagues!

I realized that I was always very tired after lunch in the afternoon, that I could not concentrate that much on my work. This began to be different then. I was not tired, I was fresh as in the morning and had my cup of coffee, but only for the taste of it.

I also became used to my rolled oates and when I skipped them for the sake of a birthday lunch – that are just a few in the year – I was sorry.

I think I love my rolled oates, I have finally found a way to integrate a way of eating less in a healthy way into my life. This also does not disturb my family life, my family dinner or my lunches and dinners at weekends.

Perhaps you find a different way for yourself! I think the most important thing is to be consequent and to change something in one's eating habits not just for a short time but for a longer period, even for ever.

Anyway, I hope it was delightful to read for you and you get out the next station in a good mood! Anyway, don't forget to consult your doctor if you bear in mind to change your eating habits or diet.

I wish you a pleasant journey
– a journey home, a journey to work,
a journey through your life!

Bless you and me!